A Curston Ranch Christmas

Curston Ranch Series Novella

Lacy Chantell

Contents

Copyrights V

Dedication VI

Acknowledgements VII

1. Chapter One 1

2. Chapter Two 4

3. Chapter Three 9

4. Chapter Four 12

5. Chapter Five 16

6. Chapter Six 19

7. Chapter Seven 23

8. Chapter Eight 29

9. Chapter Nine 33

10. Chapter Ten 38

11. Chapter Eleven 43

12. Chapter Twelve 47

13. Chapter Thirteen 52

14. Chapter Fourteen 57
15. Chapter Fifteen 62
16. Chapter Sixteen 69
17. Chapter Seventeen 74
18. Chapter Eighteen 81
19. Chapter Nineteen 85
20. Chapter Twenty 90
Afterword 95
About the author 96
Also by 97

Dedication

To my readers.

You guys are simply the best.

Acknowledgements

For all my Curston Ranch lovers who have read my books, recommended my books, and purchased my books. This is the last piece of their story I've been dying to share. You will see these characters in future books within this world and I have sprinkled some easter eggs for you throughout this Christmas novella.

Thank you from the bottom of my heart. None of this would have been possible without you.

Chapter One

THE FIRE CRACKLES FROM the hearth in the cabin. There's something about wood heat in the dead of winter that has Marni completely at peace. Having Connor tracing delicate patterns on her heated skin helps too.

He kisses her shoulder, and she sighs, sinking deeper into the pillow and on the verge of sleep.

"I have to go." His breath ghosts across her skin, and she snuggles in closer to him at her back.

"No," she says with a pout.

Connor chuckles and wraps his arm tightly around her body, holding her close.

"Not all of us get to call into work on a snow day," he teases.

She weaves her fingers with his and holds on tight. "Give me a few minutes and I'll go with you," she says, less than thrilled about being outside in the frigid temperatures.

"City life has made you soft, Mar."

She scoffs and elbows him back. "I am not soft!" Rolling over, she shoves him to his back and places her hands on his shoulders. "Take it back."

Connor laughs and cups her cheek, brushing his thumb against her skin. "You are many, many incredible things. But no, you're far from soft. You're resilient, a fighter. You don't back down when things get hard...even when I wish you would like when some lunatic is trying to kill my sister."

His head falls back into the pillow and he closes his eyes. It's been several months since he thought he lost her and his sister on the same night. The nightmares of Marni, bloodied and shot on the floor, happen less and less, but he's never been so scared in his entire life.

"Hey," she says softly, pulling him back into his peaceful cabin. Her fingers brush his lips and her dark chocolate eyes stare down at him. "I love you. I'm right here. We are okay," she reminds him.

He takes a deep breath and kisses her fingertips. "I know. I love you so much it hurts, Mar." He offers a small smile and tucks her hair behind her ear. "I'm very late. I have to go."

She quickly kisses his lips and slips out from under the warm cocoon of blankets they've been bundled in. Her skin pebbles from the chilled floor in the bathroom as she brushes her teeth and pulls on her thermals before her jeans and shirt. Connor gets dressed much quicker and starts the truck. He leans on the doorway for the bathroom, watching Marni tie her wild rag around her neck and shrugging on her jacket and felt cowboy hat.

"What?" she asks, suddenly self-conscious and double checking herself in the mirror.

"I'm the luckiest guy in the world," he says sweetly, his blue eyes hidden by the brim of his cowboy hat.

Her cheeks redden, and she looks away from him.

"Marni," Connor purrs, stepping forward and tipping her chin up. "Don't do that. Not with me. You are beautiful and I am so lucky to have you. Don't hide from me." His thumb brushes across her bottom lip and she places her hands on his forearm.

"I'm sorry," she says and nods when he doesn't break away from her gaze. "C'mon." She takes his hand in hers. "We have work to do."

They follow the ruts in the snow from the cabin to the barn and as they pass Tonya's cabin, Connor lies on the horn at the sight of Hocks' truck still parked in the driveway.

Marni playfully swats at his arm, and Connor grins. "At least I won't be the one getting shit for showing up after the sun is up."

Chapter Two

"SHIT," HOCKS MUTTERS BETWEEN Tonya's thighs. He knows the honk from outside was Connor and Hocks is officially late.

"Don't you dare stop," Tonya says through panting breaths. Steam from the hot shower fills her refinished bathroom and her legs drape over Hocks' shoulders. His fingers dig into her ass while he sucks and bites on her clit.

"Don't stop!" she laments as her fingers thread through his brown wavy hair. Her thighs clench around his head as she cries out her orgasm, and he keeps her flush against the bathroom wall. Once her body relaxes under his hands, he slowly drops her legs off his shoulders and grins up at her from his knees.

"Connor is going to bust your balls," she teases, quickly washing the proof of what they just did off her body.

"He knows what happens when someone tells you no," Hocks says and pushes to his feet, running his head under the hot stream of water and washing his short beard and unkept hair.

Tonya smirks and steps out of the shower to dry off, pulling her hair free and braiding it down her back. Hocks turns the water off and finds Tonya almost fully dressed and finishing her lukewarm cup of coffee.

"I would have been on time if you didn't hold me hostage," Hocks grumbles, pulling on his briefs and jeans.

"I'll be sure and let him know you caved at the sight of my fingers between my legs and that I didn't even have to hogtie you to *hold you hostage*."

Hocks slaps her ass as she walks by and she giggles. "You certainly will not tell him any of that."

He fills his thermos and accepts that his time in the shower with Tonya cost him hot coffee. Totally worth it.

"You better hurry or you're going to be walking!" Tonya shouts with a joking tone, and Piper jumps off the couch, racing out the door.

"Shit!" Hocks grumbles when he can't get the lid of his thermos on right and coffee spills onto the floor.

"Darlin', you just cost me liquid gold! You're going to pay for that!" Hocks appears on the porch just as Tonya fires up the truck and backs out of the driveway.

Her smile couldn't be any wider in the truck as she laughs at the sight of Hocks running after her with a grin of his own down the snowy road.

Once she's laughed so hard her stomach hurts, she presses the brake and Hocks wrenches open the driver's door.

His cheeks are flushed red and his green eyes can't hide the humor as they sparkle.

"Just wait until tonight," he says with dark promise, and Tonya gives him a salacious smile.

"Promise?"

Hocks shakes his head and Tonya slides across the bench seat and he climbs in behind the steering wheel. He grabs her chin and pulls her in for a kiss, their hats pushing up their foreheads. "God, I love you, darlin'. More and more every day."

"Good, because you're stuck with me, Stud." Tonya raises her hand and her engagement ring sparkles in the early morning sun. "Just one month until you take my last name, and it'll officially be yours."

Hocks takes her hand in his and kisses her ring finger, then puts the truck in drive.

"And you'll be mine forever."

Piper barks excitedly from the truck bed as they pull up to the barn. She waits for Hocks to give her the signal to jump out, then she races inside the barn.

"I'm yours with or without the paperwork, Hocks," Tonya says, her voice holding vulnerability that she reserves only for him.

He pushes her against the truck and takes her mouth with his, shoving every emotion he feels for her into this kiss.

Derek is gone.

The ranch is safe.

This is his life and his home.

Tonya is his home.

And in one month he'll be getting married alongside his best friend for a double wedding.

“You’re late!” Connor shouts from the barn. He holds Clover’s reins in his hands and Marni steps up beside him with Orion.

She smiles are her best friend and future sister, lightly slapping Connor on the shoulder.

“Hocks had to have his breakfast first. Marni, did Connor have *breakfast* before he came down? Is that why he’s so grumpy?” Tonya shouts and Hocks’ mouth hangs open.

“Tonya!” Hocks hisses.

Connor’s features twist, and he shakes his head, turning his back on his best friend. “Get your ass in a saddle. We promised Ma we’d be back to decorate for Christmas.”

“You could hogtie me in a red ribbon and put me under the tree,” Tonya whispers to Hocks before sauntering into the barn.

He stares after her for a beat, then he takes a moment to gaze across the ranch. The Curstons will never truly know how much they changed his life.

He's at peace. No longer looking over his shoulder or wondering if his past will catch up with him at every turn.

For the first time in Hocks' life, he's going to have a family Christmas.

Family.

He has a family.

Chapter Three

CHRISTMAS MUSIC FILLS THE farmhouse as Stacy places the garland on the mantel and hangs mistletoe between the kitchen and living room.

Jack carries box after box of Christmas decorations from the attic and the last one lands with a thud and he groans as he straightens his back.

"Stace, do you really need all of this stuff? I can't remember the last time I saw some of these boxes."

"Really need?" she squawks. "Jack! It's Christmas and *all* my kids are home for the first time in ten years. There won't be a single place left bare after I'm done. Then, on Christmas Day, we will all settle in the fire and eat a family meal. Oh, Jack!" she sighs. "This is what I've been waiting my whole life for!"

His demeanor softens, and he walks up behind his wife.

"Then we'll make it look like St. Nick threw up all over this place," he says, nuzzling her neck.

She swats him away with her hand. "Both our babies are engaged and getting married. I want everything to be special."

Jack spins her to face him and wraps his arms around her waist. "It'll be special, sweetheart. I can promise you that. But the decorations have nothing to do with it."

She arches a brow and gives him the look he knows well. She isn't budging, and he's about to spend the entire day decorating his house.

"You can start with the tree," she states, and points to the corner of the living room.

"I figured," he says, kissing her nose and grabbing the large box. "Honestly, I'm surprised you're not making me go cut down a damn tree to put in here."

He drops the box and straightens, glancing at his wife out of the corner of his eye. Immediately, he regrets his statement.

"Stace, no. No. Don't give me that look. Absolutely not."

Stacy nods, ignoring her husband's objections, and sets the strand of lights she had in her hands on the table.

"Jack Curston, you're a genius! I'm going to change. Get your keys and coat. We're going to find us a *real* Christmas Tree."

Her eyes sparkle as she smiles wide and rushes upstairs to their bedroom.

Jack runs a hand through his graying hair. "You just had to open your damn mouth," he grumbles and yanks his jacket off the coat rack. "You couldn't just leave her alone with all her decorations and you just made this ten times worse on yourself. Cutting down a tree in the middle of winter," he scoffs.

When Stacy steps onto the porch with her felt cowboy hat snug down on her head and a wild rag tied neatly around her neck, he's taken back to the first Christmas they had in their new home.

Susan and Sammy sat around with Susan's parents and he thought that was the best Christmas he could have. Then he had Connor, and he didn't think it got better than that. Then they had Tonya, then Marni would join. Now with his kids engaged and a wedding around the corner, just when he thinks it can't get any better, it does.

"Are you going to stand there gawking all day? We don't have much time and I don't want the Millers to be sold out. We've almost waited too long!"

"Rattlesnake," Jack says as she rushes up to him. "I love you."

Her lips part and she blinks up at him. "You haven't called me that in years," she whispers.

"I just thought of our first Christmas in our new home. We've come so far from a broken bull rider and a mouthy girl from Florida."

He grabs her hand as she scoffs and tries to turn away.

"We're going to find you the perfect tree, sweetheart." He kisses her hand, and she melts into him.

"Thank you, Jack. And I love you, too. More and more every day."

Chapter Four

Jack watches Stacy as she runs her fingers along the needles of the last pine tree at Millers Tree Farm. The sparkle that shone in her eyes back at the ranch has been snuffed out to defeat.

"Maybe once we add lights and the ornaments, it'll look..." He tilts his head to the side and tries to find a side of the tree that doesn't look like it belongs in the Charlie Brown story.

"It's no use, Jack. We waited too long. I can't take this home. I'll have to settle for the fake tree. I mean, there's nothing wrong with it. It's fine. The idea of a real tree for Christmas just made it feel more special."

He wraps his arms around her shoulders and rubs a hand up and down her arm. "It's not about the tree, sweetheart. It was a good idea."

She laughs and gazes up at him. "I know you don't mean that, but thank you. I guess we should head home before the whole day is a bust."

Jack nods and watches Stacy out of his periphery as he drives. He racks his brain, trying to come up with a solution to give Stacy her dream Christmas.

Once they're back at the ranch, he lets Stacy out at the farmhouse, then drives over to the barn with an idea.

"Connor? Can you hear me?" Jack asks into his phone.

Connor turns his back to the wind and tries to make out what Jack is asking.

"You want us to what?" he asks, and Marni rides up next to him, their knees brushing.

Connor looks around the snow-covered landscape and waves his hand. "Everything is covered in snow." He sighs and drops his chin. "No, no. Don't do that. I'll—we'll figure something out...yeah, total surprise."

He disconnects the call and Hocks and Tonya ride closer. "Who was that?" Tonya asks.

"That was Dad. Mom wants a real tree to decorate and Millers' was sold out." Connor taps his heels against his horse's side and they ride down the fence line, checking for weak spots or holes.

"What are we supposed to do about it?" Tonya asks. "Go cut her one?" She means it as a joke, but the way Connor looks at the group tells her that's exactly what they're going to do.

"Okay, so we...what? Everything is covered in snow and there isn't a way to get the truck up here to haul one back," Marni states.

"That's why we'll be using horses and a sled. Which means we have to ride back to the barn, get a chainsaw, pony a horse out and find the perfect tree for this Christmas," Connor says like all of that is an easy feat.

"This is certainly a first," Marni says with a chuckle. She doesn't say it out loud, but the thought of a real tree brings her inner child to the surface. It's been ten years since she's had a Curston Ranch Christmas. For the past five years, she's been alone in her apartment with Ginger.

The five years before that her parents didn't decorate or acknowledge there was even a holiday.

"Why don't we split up? A couple of us will go pick out the perfect tree while the others meet up with the horse and chainsaw. Cut our time down," Hocks offers.

"We can go back," Tonya supplies. "You two go find our tree." She jerks her chin at Connor and Marni.

Her best friend's eyes light up and she glances at Connor, who looks less than enthused.

"Try to smile, brother. It's festive," Tonya teases and nudges Hocks with her leg to follow her to the barn.

Marni rides alongside Connor as they continue to follow the fence line. "You know, this is my first Christmas since I left," she breathes. He glances over at her. He hadn't even thought about what this Christmas means to her. For him it's the same thing every year, but for the woman he loves—he can't fathom what her normal was.

He holds his gloved hand out, and she takes it, holding her reins in the other.

"Then we're going to find the best damn tree on this ranch and make this the best Christmas you've ever had."

She smiles at him, the tip of her nose and cheeks red. "The bar for the *best* is set pretty low. Simply waking up with you on Christmas makes it the best ever, Connor. You don't have to do anything special for me."

He clucks his horse up to a trot and smiles. "You're right, I don't *have* to. But I want to spoil you and I'm going to. Think you can keep up? I have an idea where we'll find the perfect tree."

Chapter Five

TONYA SLIDES THE CHAINSAW into the leather case on the side of her saddle while Hocks secures the harness on a sorrel gelding.

"You probably think this is ridiculous," Tonya jokes as she stands back and watches Hocks. "It's cheesy, sure, but--"

"I don't think it's ridiculous," Hocks supplies, cutting Tonya off. She tilts her head to the side and furrows her brows.

"Really? The lights, mistletoe, hot chocolate, Christmas music, a live tree...none of this seems over the top to you?"

Hocks tightens the last strap and stands to face Tonya. "My mom didn't have any family, as you can imagine. She only focused on the next score and brought men home who paid her. As you know, my foster care situation wasn't any better. I've never had a family Christmas, T. I've never done the lights, presents, trees, or kissed under mistletoe. I don't think any of it is ridiculous...and you shouldn't either."

Tonya's lips part and her eyes well with tears at the image of a young Hocks alone on Christmas.

In three long strides, she wraps her arms around him and squeezes. She rapidly blinks back the tears before they escape.

"Don't go feeling sorry for me," he states. "I wouldn't trade any of it because it brought me here. But to be honest, I'm really excited to go cut a real tree and decorate with you."

"You haven't seen Stacy Curston decorate yet. You may regret the enthusiasm," Tonya teases into his chest.

"Not a chance. Let's go find us a tree."

They find Connor and Marni deep in a thicket of pine trees. The horses are tied beside the perfectly symmetrical evergreen that is full and doesn't have a single bare spot. It stands shorter than the ones around it, shielding it from the relentless snow.

"It's perfect," Tonya states, having a whole new perspective on Christmas with her family. Marni walks over as the guys pull out the chainsaw and make a plan on which way is best to cut it.

"I thought so, too! This is so exciting. I can't wait to see how it looks all decorated in your parents' living room."

Tonya tugs on her best friend's hand and they step away from hearing distance. "Did you get everything you need for Connor's present?" she asks.

Marni glances at the men and the chainsaw revs to life. "I think so. I'm so nervous though! What about you? Did you decide on something for Hocks?"

Tonya chews on her bottom lip. "Nothing feels like enough. Especially since this is his first family Christmas...like ever! How did I not realize how critical this is?" she whisper-shouts.

"Okay, calm down. No need to panic. He doesn't strike me as the type who cares about the gift as much as he does the person giving it to him. But if you're really worried, we can go to town tomorrow and do some last-minute shopping. It'll be fine."

"Easy for you to say. You have the *perfect* gift."

Marni gives her a sad smile. "T, he loves you and he'll love whatever you get him."

"Timber!" Hocks shouts as the tree pops and cracks. It falls with a vibrating thud and the horses prance where they're tied.

The women clap and cheer at a job well done, then lead the sorrel gelding to the tree for Hocks and Connor to hook it up.

Connor and Marni lead and pony the harnessed horse, with Hocks and Tonya following behind.

It's a slow ride back to the farmhouse and across the snowy ranch. Their group is a vision of something from a hallmark movie on their way to give Stacy the best gift she could ever imagine.

Chapter Six

JACK SMILES AT THE sight through the kitchen window by the barn.

"Stace!" he shouts through the house and she rushes in with flustered cheeks and her hair falling around her face.

"What's wrong? What is it?"

She glances around the kitchen looking for a fire or water everywhere, but nothing is amiss.

"Close your eyes, sweetheart. I have a surprise for you." Jack spins her around and places his hands over her eyes.

"What are you doing? Christmas isn't until this weekend."

Jack gently kisses the crown of her head and smiles. "Trust me."

The cold air pebbles her skin as they step onto the porch. "No peeking!" Tonya shouts when Stacy places her hands over Jack's.

"What is this?" she asks. "What are you all planning?"

"Merry Christmas, sweetheart," Jack whispers and lets his hands fall away.

Connor and Hocks stand in the snow holding the sides of the Christmas tree and Marni and Tonya bounce on their toes in excitement.

"You—it's—oh, Jack." Tears well in Stacy's eyes and she lifts her hand to her trembling lips. "It's perfect," she says, her throat tightening. Tonya and Marni climb the porch steps and Stacy pulls them both in for a hug.

"This means so much," Stacy whispers.

"We didn't do anything. Hocks and Connor did all the work," Tonya supplies and gestures to her brother and fiancé.

"Thank you both," Stacy says, dabbing her eyes. "This is why you refused to get up and help me with the tree. Was the sink really broken?" she asks Jack and everyone laughs.

"Well, I wasn't about to decorate one just to decorate this one," Jack defends. "Are you going to make them boys stand there holding it until Christmas, or are you going to bark orders and tell them where to put it?"

Stacy puts her hands on her hips and arches a brow at her husband. "I don't bark," she states, and Jack laughs.

"No, rattlesnake. You are all bite."

Tonya and Marni glance at each other in confusion.

"Rattlesnake?" Tonya asks. "You know what? I don't even want to know." She waves her hand and goes inside to shed off her layer of clothes.

"This is going to be the best Christmas ever," Marni tells Stacy as she walks inside.

"Yes it is, dear." Stacy squeezes Marni's hand and wipes her eyes as her live tree is carried inside.

Hours later, everyone stands back as Stacy holds the extension cord. "Moment of truth," she says with excitement.

Every ornament found a place and Marni and Hocks heard every childhood Christmas story Stacy and Jack could think of.

Connor wraps his arm around Marni and pulls her into his side while Tonya rests her head on Hocks' chest beside them.

The tree lights up and warms the room in a yellow glow of twinkling lights. There is something calming about a lit tree and Marni sighs against Connor.

"It's better than I remember," she whispers and he tightens his hold, making a silent promise right there that every Christmas will be like this for the woman he loves.

Tonya gazes up at Hocks, the lights reflecting in his green iris'. He stares at the tree in awe. Never has he decorated for Christmas as a family. The closest thing he ever had as a tree was the year one of his mom's boyfriends brought in a pine sapling so he could play family for the holidays.

He feels Tonya staring at him and he looks down at her. How he got so lucky to have all of this, he'll never know.

Stacy stares at her tree full of memories. From her and Jack's first Christmas, to her babies' firsts', and all the ones to follow. She and Jack didn't inherit memories from their parents, and she certainly didn't inherit any from her aunt and uncle. This tree symbolizes their life and moments that have sculpted everything they've built today.

Her gaze sweeps across the room to her daughter and Hocks, then her son and Marni. Last, she stares at the man who loved her enough for both of them and never gave up.

For a moment she's transported back to the night she walked into the Becketts barn after he told her he loved her. His gray hair and wrinkles are gone, and he's staring at her like she's the only person in the room.

Like Marni said, this is going to be the best Christmas ever.

Chapter Seven

"So are your parents coming for Christmas?" Tonya asks Marni as they browse through Haney Tack Shop.

"You know Mom. She's so busy, but she'll try to make it." Marni tries to not let it bother her; she knows it shouldn't. It's been like this her whole life, but this year is different and she really wishes she would attempt to come.

"And the wedding?" Tonya asks hesitantly.

Marni doesn't have to answer. Her best friend knows it's the same speech. Still, if she shows up, she'll have a corsage as the mother of the bride.

"Anyway," Marni says. "Do you see anything that screams at you that Hocks would like or need?"

Tonya has sifted through every corner of this shop, and nothing has caught her eye. "I don't know," she whines, hating that she's feeling like this.

"Okay, well, does he need a new belt? You could have his name engraved? Or a new set of spurs? A saddle? Anything?"

Tonya huffs and shrugs. "I don't know. He never complains, never says he wants anything."

Marni smiles. "Because he has everything he could ever want," she coos, and her best friend rolls her eyes.

"Not helping." She gets a panicked wild look in her eyes and Marni takes a step closer to her friend.

"T, it's okay. Hocks doesn't care about this stuff. Why are you freaking out?"

"Because this is his first real Christmas and I want it to be special for him. He deserves something thoughtful and sentimental."

Marni hugs her best friend. "Then we'll find the perfect gift. We still have time."

Tonya looks around the tack shop and tries to think of something—anything that her cowboy would like.

Across the shop, steam rises from the branding iron as it presses into a felt cowboy hat. Tonya grips her best friend's hand.

"He'll officially have a family after we say I do. He'll be a Curston, and that means so much to him."

"Yeah," Marni says. "I know how he feels."

Tonya's blue eyes crinkle with her knowing smile. "I know exactly what I'm getting him."

***

THE RANCH IS QUIET with the freshly fallen snow that covers every surface. Connor steps onto the porch of his cabin while Marni still sleeps bundled under three comforters. He added fresh wood to the stove this morning after being up most of the night. Once he realized the significance of Christmas traditions for Marni, he made the decision to do something he's never done before.

He walks into his cabin and grins at his hard work. He can't wait to see Marni's reaction.

Cold hands slide under her blanket and Marni squirms when they glide across her skin. Connor's fingers dip between her thighs and she squeals, sitting upright and nearly colliding with her smiling fiancé.

"Good morning," he purrs, and she rubs her eyes.

"What time is it?" she asks, glancing at the clock on the table beside their bed. "It's not even daylight! Why are you dressed?"

"I have a surprise for you." He kisses her nose and straightens, holding his hand out to her.

"Christmas is tomorrow," she says skeptically.

He doesn't falter, and she wraps the comforter around her as she stands.

"Close your eyes," he says as he guides her out of the bedroom into the living space.

"Connor," she giggles and takes tentative steps across the hardwood floor.

"Merry Christmas, Marni," he whispers and she opens her eyes.

Her lips part at the sight of their cabin. A fully decorated tree sits in the corner, its soft yellow glow illuminating the wooden walls of the room. Lit garland decorates the mantle and door frame of their house.

She spins, her expression a mixture of shock and awe only to find Connor with a red Santa hat on his head. Her eyes are filled with unshed tears and she burst out with laughter at the sight of her fiancé.

"You are full of surprises, Mr. Curston," she says. "Thank you."

"Anything for you, Mar. Let me show you how much I love you," he says.

"Does the Santa hat stay on?"

He smirks and the lights reflect in his blue eyes as he unbuttons his shirt and pants. "Anything for you," he repeats, and Marni lets the comforter fall to the floor.

Connor slips free of his briefs and lifts Marni in his arms, carrying her to the couch.

"Something wrong with the bed?" she teases as she straddles him.

Connor skims his fingers over her delicate collarbone and down to her pebbled nipples. "I did all this work and I want to enjoy it with you like this."

The Christmas lights cast caramel highlights down her long brown hair and he runs his fingers through the strands, then down her back to settle on her hips. "I love how you look on my lap with the flames from the hearth dancing across your skin."

Marni threads her fingers through his blond hair at his nape and dips down to press her lips to his. "I love you, Connor Curston," she says against his lips.

"Show me," he teases.

She scoffs, then leans down and deepens the kiss and takes her other hand to line his cock up with her center. She lowers herself until she's fully seated and her head falls back at how amazing he feels.

His fingers dig into her hips as she rocks back and forth, her breasts bouncing with the movement and he pulls her nipple into his mouth, then moves to the other one, rolling it between his teeth. The white furry ball from his hat tickles her skin.

"Merry Christmas Eve, Santa," she says through heavy breaths, placing her hands on his shoulders and gazing down at him.

"I think this will be a new tradition for us." He kisses her collarbone, then lifts her from his lap and slams her back down while thrusting his hips. Marni cries out, her nails digging into his skin. Connor slams her down again, then grips her ass and grinds her against him. Her breath quickens as her orgasm coils and fights to be set free.

He never saw himself as a man with holiday traditions. He always took the family dinners and celebrating for granted. With Marni, he's seeing it all in a new light and realizing just how precious it all really is.

His legs tense as he buries himself fully inside of her. She moans as she comes and falls forward to rest her forehead on his shoulder. Connor pistons himself up, and Marni cries out with his rough movements.

"Yes," she mewls, digging her nails into his shoulders as Connor groans through gritted teeth and his body tenses under her.

He wraps his arms around her and pulls her against his chest, allowing himself a few more moments of bliss.

Marni's eyes flutter closed from the warmth of his skin against hers. She'll never be able to thank Tonya enough for getting her back on this ranch. This is her home and in just a couple of months she'll get to ride down the aisle and say 'I Do'.

She's nearly asleep when Connor's hand brushes down her spine.

"C'mon," he says softly. "We have more festivities to tend to today and we can't be late."

"More festive than you decorating our cabin for me?" Marni asks, but instead of answering, he carries her to the shower.

Chapter Eight

CONNOR HAS MARNI IN the truck just as the sun crests the mountains. After she repeatedly asked what they're doing and him ignoring the question, she gave up and stares at him from the passenger seat.

To her surprise, he pulls into Tonya and Hocks driveway and honks the horn.

"We're all going?"

Connor nods. "If they get their asses in the truck in the next five minutes."

Tonya rushes out the door laughing and smiling with Hocks on her heels. She beats on the back of Marni's seat.

"This year is it! Ain't nobody going to beat us with Marni in the saddle. You just wait!"

Connor glances at her through the rear-view mirror.

"Will someone please tell me what is going on? Where are we going and why will I be in a saddle? Are we taking the horses?" Marni turns sideways in her seat. "Well?"

Tonya looks at her brother. "You haven't told her?"

He shakes his head. "I was going to let you."

Marni raises her brows expectantly and Tonya's smile widens. She resembles a giddy child who can't hold in her excitement.

"It's the annual Cowboy Winter Games, and you are my partner, which means we're going to kick some ass!" Tonya places her hand on Marni's shoulder and shakes her.

"They're still doing that?!" Marni's brown eyes light up and she glances to Connor, then back to her best friend.

"Yes!"

Connor and Hocks share a knowing look. Marni doesn't hold back and Tonya doesn't know fear.

Today is going to be one to remember.

White plumes billow from the horse's nostrils as they unload him from the trailer. Marni runs a hand down Playboy's head and he shifts his attention to the crowds and other horses.

The whole town seems to be there, and she lost count of how many trailers are parked.

It's been years since she and Tonya came down here the year Tonya got her license.

"Taking in your competition?" Tonya asks Marni.

"Just getting in touch with Playboy before I ask him to run his heart out."

"He's a good boy. He'll take care of us." Tonya pats his side.

"It's been years, T. Are you sure about this?"

"Just like old times, Mar. You run. Don't hold back and I won't let go."

Tonya bumps her shoulder with her best friend and they both smile.

"I guess we should go draw our number, then."

Hocks and Connor follow close behind as they immerse into the crowd of locals, careful to not let their women get out of their sights. What happened with Derek is too fresh in both of their minds for that.

"Are we sure this was a good idea?" Hocks mutters under his breath so Tonya doesn't hear. "The last thing we need is an ER trip on Christmas Eve. I'm pretty sure your mom would kill us."

Connor chuckles. "Do you really think we're the reason they're here? No. Those two women would have come even if we didn't. We're here to make sure we don't end up in the hospital. I mean, my girl will be safe on the back of a horse. Yours? That's a different story."

Hocks groans and rolls his eyes. "Shit."

Connor clasps his shoulder. "Good luck, man."

Marni bounces on her toes and Tonya writes their name on the list.

"Nervous?" Connor whispers as he places a kiss on her temple.

Marni's eyes glow as he looks up at him. "Not even close. I'm so excited."

He smirks and places his hands in his pockets. "We aren't teenagers anymore, Mar. Just...be careful."

"Are you...worried about me?" she asks, her eyes widening and a playful smirk tilts her lips.

"Nah, of course not. I've seen you ride. But if either of you come home with bruises or a cast, Mom will kill me. And you haven't seen her mad until something messes with Christmas."

"Oh brother," Tonya says, slapping Connor's back. "You have nothing to worry about. This is just a little bit of festive fun! Why don't you go see Susan's truck and get us some drinks while we get ready?" She quickly kisses Hocks' cheek, then pulls Marni back to the trailers.

"Don't let him get in your head, Mar. It's just running. Nothing else to it."

"I'm not worried about Playboy and me at all. Connor, on the other hand seems to have enough worry for all of us."

Tonya rolls her eyes. "I'm pretty sure Hocks tried to fuck the idea of coming here today out of me all. Night. Long."

Marni shoves at her friend. "T!" she squeals.

She shrugs. "It didn't work, though. There is no way I'd let your first Christmas home pass by without doing this. It's a tradition."

"Sledding, skiing, and snowboarding with added horsepower. What more can a girl want?"

Chapter Nine

Playboy snorts and drops his head as Marni adjusts her reins. Connor keeps a hand on her thigh as they wait their turn to race down the snowy course. Hocks and Tonya stand on the opposite side with a rope and sled.

"Do you enjoy making my heart beat out of my chest?" Hocks asks, staring at the horse as it races down the course, dragging a rider on a sled behind it.

"It is very cute how your brows pinch," Tonya teases as she pokes Hocks' forehead.

The crowd collectively gasps as the rider on the sled flies off mid jump and lands in the snow.

Hocks grabs Tonya's hand and squeezes. His grip doesn't relax until the sledder stands and pumps a fist into the air.

"He's probably too drunk to feel anything," she shrugs. She faces her fiancé and pulls her hand free and cups his cheek. "I love you, Stud."

He shakes his head and tries to snatch her hand as she walks alongside Playboy and approaches the starting line.

Marni takes a deep breath and gathers her reins. She glances over her shoulder as Tonya places the sled on the snow and positions herself on plastic. She pulls goggles over her head and hands her hat off to Hocks.

"Don't let go!" Marni shouts.

"Don't hold back!" Tonya responds.

They can't stop the smiles that spread across their faces while Hocks looks like he's forgotten how to breathe.

A fog horn blares and Marni digs her heels in and kicks Playboy up to a full gallop from a standstill. The rope snags tight and Tonya's lurched forward, but Marni can't risk looking behind her to see if she's still on. She has to trust her best friend means is when she said she won't let go.

Her heart thunders in her chest as Playboy gallops as fast as he can across the snowy ground.

Tonya tightens her grip as they take the first curve and the sled drifts around sideways. The first jump is coming up, and she tenses every muscle in her body to keep her stuck to the sled.

She slides up the icy surface and launches into the air, her stomach free falling into her back and she holds her breath until she lands with a resounding thud on the hard plastic. The air is knocked from her lungs, but she doesn't have time to recover before she's airborne again.

If it wasn't for the goggles, she wouldn't be able to see through the icy air. Playboy kicks up snow with each stride and Marni leans forward, so close it's as if she's melding with the horse. Tonya's hand nearly slips, but she recovers, her heart beating against her ribcage. One more jump and she's in the clear.

Marni takes the curve, the rope attached to the horn, rubs on her leg, reminding her that Tonya is still back there. It's the home stretch, one more jump.

"Come on, Playboy," she encourages, slinging her reins to get him to go faster, to ask for every ounce of his heart.

Tonya drifts around the curve and doesn't have time to straighten before she hits the jump and the sled tilts. The rope goes slack as she slingshots faster than Playboy is running. She grits her teeth, preparing for the worst, and debates for one second of letting go. But she's stubborn and not a quitter. If there's an inkling of a chance she'll stick this landing and not roll, she'll try it.

Mid-air, the rope snags and jerks, straightening the sled, and Tonya is slung to the side. One leg hangs off the edge of the sled and her hands scream from the strain as her shoulders pull to keep her body on the sled.

Too quickly, she lands in the snow, and her leg drags along the icy ground beside her. She rolls to her side, keeping her grip.

“Run!” she shouts, although she’s not sure Marni can hear her over the roar of the wind and cheers of the crowd.

Connor and Hocks push through the crowd to reach Marni and Tonya as they slide past the finish line. Marni pulls Playboy back to a slow stop and Tonya rolls over on the sled.

“T!” Hocks shouts, worry and panic in his voice. He crouches, pulling the goggles from her face, and Tonya takes deep breaths, her hands shaking slightly.

“That was...”

“Insane, reckless, stupid, dangerous and terrifying?” Hocks supplies.

Tonya laughs and pumps her fists into the air. “Amazing! Did we win?!”

Her fiancé groans and hauls Tonya to her feet. “Darlin’, are you actively trying to give me a heart attack?”

Connor pulls Marni from the saddle and holds her tight, kissing her in front of everyone with so much passion her cheeks heat.

When he pulls back, she blinks up at him, head spinning from adrenaline and having the daylight kissed out of her.

“What was that for?” she asks.

“I remember why I hated going to the rodeos. I was always terrified of seeing you get hurt. That shit is hard to fucking watch.”

She tilts her head and gazes up at him. “I run on the ranch all the time,” she says.

Connor shakes his head. “I know. It’s different from watching you compete. Even at something like this.” He waves his hands behind him.

“So, are you saying I can’t compete in team roping again?” she asks, batting her eyelashes.

“I’d never tell you, you can’t do something, Mar.” He takes a deep breath and grabs Playboy’s reins to lead him through the crowd and back to the trailer. “I’ll just have to get some high blood pressure medicine.”

Chapter Ten

"Hey boss!" Lucas says as he approaches with Wes. "That's a mighty fine trophy you got there." He points to the wooden carved trophy in Tonya's hands and she smiles.

"Don't tell me we beat you too?" she teases.

Wes claps his hand on Lucas' shoulder. "Somebody couldn't hang on through the last jump," Wes says and Lucas' cheeks turn as red as his hair.

"Shut up, man. You can't ride straight."

They all laugh. "I'm going to miss having you around, Wes. It won't be the same without you on the ranch. You're a hard worker, I mean that." Connor praises and Wes stares at him with wide, unbelieving eyes.

"Thank you, sir. That means a lot."

"I'm sure we'll be seeing you in...what? Eight years?" Tonya asks.

Wes nods. "When I open my practice, I hope I'll have ya'll as clients."

Connor hugs Marni into his chest. It's still surreal to him he's planning a future with her at his side. In less than a month, she'll be his wife and in eight years, she'll still be at his ranch and he'll be loving her every day.

"We'd love that," Tonya says with a smile, pulling Connor back to the conversation.

"If you need anything, you call us. Okay?" he tells Wes.

"I will." Wes beams at Connor, Hocks, Tonya, and Marni. Working on Curston Ranch has been some of the best times for him. He almost decided against going to university because he couldn't picture himself anywhere else. But he wants to make the Curstons proud and to come back one day and be their veterinarian would be a dream.

"Hey," Lucas says, punching Wes in the shoulder. "We don't have time for goodbyes. Not here. These two are our competition, remember? Don't let them get into your head and make you all mushy. This ain't over."

Tonya raises the trophy. "It looks pretty over," she teases, and Lucas scoffs.

"Okay, okay. We'll see you guys out there," Marni says, gently guiding Tonya toward the horse trailer. "Good luck!" she calls over her shoulder.

"Do you even know how to ski, T? Have you done it before?" Hocks asks, worry lacing his tone.

"No, but how hard can it be?"

Marni steps in front of her. "We're not skiing. We're getting married in 2 weeks, T. What happens if you break a leg? You got a trophy. We won. It was fun, but we should really stop while we're ahead."

Tonya's mouth falls open, and she glances from her fortified brother behind her best friend and her fiancé. "Are you ganging up on me? Marni, you're supposed to be on my side!"

"Don't be ridiculous. I simply want you in one piece when we walk down the aisle," her best friend says softly.

"Same," Hocks agrees. "We have things to do on our wedding night that I need you in tip-top shape for."

"Shit, man. Why? Why did you have to go there?" Connor groans.

Hocks winks at Tonya and shrugs. "I'm hoping my tongue can persuade her to leave."

"Nope. I'm done. I'm not listening to this." Connor takes Marni's hand and pulls her toward Playboy to load up. "She's your problem now, since you put that ring on her finger. Figure it out," he tells Hocks.

"Are you going to let him tell you what to do?" Tonya shouts after her best friend.

Marni mouths '*sorry*', and Connor slaps her ass, making her squeal.

"I can't believe her. She turned into one of those girls who ditches her best friend when she gets a boyfriend. That's fine," Tonya says with a nod and faces Hocks. "You'll ride."

"The fuck I am. Come on, darlin'. Let's just go home. I promise to make it worth your while." His hands slide around her hips and he tugs her closer.

"Stud, I get that regardless. I want to race and if my best friend bailed on me, then I'll have to find someone else."

"Tonya, you're not doing something this dangerous," Hocks snaps and her eyes widen at his tone. "Get your ass in the truck. We're going home."

She shoves the trophy into his chest, forcing him to grab it and whirls on her heel.

"Oh fuck," Hocks grumbles and races after her.

She makes it to the registration table before he catches her.

"Tonya, are you signing up for the next event?" the woman asks.

"I'm actually in need of a partner. You wouldn't happen to know of anyone, would you?"

The woman shakes her head just as Hocks moves to stand beside her.

"T," he says softly, trying to rectify the situation.

"You need a partner?" a blonde woman asks before spitting tobacco off to the side.

"No, she doesn't," Hocks says at the same time Tonya sizes up the small woman.

"Can you run?" Tonya asks.

The woman nods. "Can you ski?"

Tonya smirks. "First time for everything."

Hocks moves to stand slightly in front of his fiancé as a pissed off cowboy with rich umber skin and mocha eyes marches toward them.

"Poss, what the hell are you doing? You ain't riding and that's final."

Hocks smirks. Clearly, this man is having the same fight he is.

"Poss?" T asks the woman.

"Short for Possum. This stick in the mud is Jed and he's harmless."

Tonya nods at the cowboy and a slow smile spreads on her lips as she sidesteps Hocks. "Well Possum, you got a horse?"

"No!" both cowboys shout in unison and the cowgirls smirk.

"Hell yeah, I got a horse," Possum responds.

"I will throw you over my shoulder in front of God and everyone," Jed warns, and Tonya waits to see how Possum responds. The blonde turns to face her cowboy and palms his crotch.

"After we win, I expect it."

Jed swats her hand away and Tonya jerks her chin toward registration.

"I'll get our names down. You warm up your horse."

"Hell yeah," Possum cheers and jogs away with Jed chasing after her.

Hocks shakes his head in defeat. The more he tells her no, the more reckless she is going to be. He knows that. By telling her to get her ass in the truck, he put this in motion. Seems Jed has a similar problem.

Chapter Eleven

Connor grips Marni's hip, pulling her into him. He tosses his hat onto the couch inside the horse trailer and shrugs out of his jacket.

"Connor," Marni giggles. "T could be back at any minute."

He kisses her neck and pulls her shirt free from her jeans, running his fingers across her soft skin. "She ain't coming back. We have plenty of time."

Marni pushes Connor back. "What do you mean? How do you know?"

He sighs. "Because Hocks told her no, which means she's definitely going to ride now. That's how she is."

"But she doesn't have a partner? What's she going to do? Find a random person?"

He shrugs. "It's what she's done every year since you've been gone. Usually finds a man to take advantage of, so I'm not sure how it'll work with her being engaged this year."

"Shit." Marni fixes her shirt and smooths her hair down. "I have to go find her before she trusts the wrong person and really gets hurt."

"Let Hocks deal with her. We can have some fun." Connor threads his fingers through hers and twirls her toward him.

Marni quickly presses her lips to his. "She's my best friend and your sister, which means her problems are our problems. Just as much as she's Hocks' problem. Come on, maybe I can talk her out of it."

The trailer door flies open, slapping against the outside and Hocks looks up at them with reddened features.

"Where's T?" Marni asks.

"Where do you think?" Hocks asks, his tone short and annoyed.

"Shit," Connor grumbles.

The three of them push their way to the starting line through the crowd of people.

"I tried talking to her. I can't watch this. Find me when she's done," Jed murmurs to another cowboy as he shoves past Hocks.

"They're up next," Hocks says and Marni pushes faster, squeezing between people easier than the cowboys.

"T!" she shouts, hoping to gain her best friend's attention. "Tonya! Wait!"

The blow horn drowns out her shouts and all they see is flying blonde and brown hair.

"T's the skier. Who's riding?" Marni asks, stretching to see over the heads of the crowd.

"Someone named Possum," Hocks supplies.

"That's one of Flynn's hands. Langley Ranch," Connor adds.

"You know her?" Marni asks.

"She's a hell of a ranch hand. Used to compete on bulls before Flynn hired her."

"So, she can ride," Marni says, her shoulders relaxing.

"Yeah, but T can't ski," Connor supplies and Marni stiffens again.

Hocks taps Connor on the shoulder. "We need to get to the finish line. Come on."

By the time they reach the line, Possum races across it, the rope dragging along the ground behind her. Hocks' heart sinks to his stomach and images of T with a broken leg, arm, or worse, penetrates his mind.

"Where is she?" Marni shouts and Hocks takes off running. Connor grabs her hand as they chase after him. No sign of Tonya.

Halfway through the course, they come up on a group huddled around, and Connor's towering form has them parting for them to get through.

"T!" Hocks shouts as he drops to his knees at her sitting in the snow, cradling her arm. His hands hover over her body like he's scared to touch her. Quickly, he unbuckles the skis from her shoes.

"Are you hurt?" Marni asks, reaching for her arm.

"It got stuck on the ring and the pole. They're supposed to slip off, ain't they?"

“Not when you twist your arm, dear,” someone from the crowd says, and Tonya scoffs.

“Darlin’, look at me.” Hocks’ voice is soft and tender and he holds his breath as she slowly lifts her gaze. “You’re okay,” he says, more to himself than to her. He helps her stand and brushes her hair from her face. “We’re taking you to the hospital. You won’t argue about it, got it?”

She gazes up at him and sighs. “Okay, Stud.”

Hock’s eyes widen. She actually listened. She didn’t argue, didn’t fight back, or try to brush him off. “Good,” he says, at a loss for words.

“Skiing is way harder than it looks,” Tonya teases.

Marni sighs and glances up at Connor. His jaw ticks, and he avoids looking at anyone as they make their way back to the truck.

Chapter Twelve

Piper whines from the porch as Hocks and Tonya climb the steps.

The dog's tail wags, and it licks at Hocks' fingertips. Once inside, Tonya collapses on the couch, her eyes falling closed.

"I'll fix something to eat," her fiancé states, walking deeper into the kitchen and pulling pans from the cabinets.

"I was thinking we could take a shower first," she offers and Hocks sighs.

"I'm hungry, T and tired from spending six hours in the ER for x-rays to show that your arm is fine."

His tone has Tonya sitting up and staring at him from over the back of the couch. "Did you prefer it was broken?"

Hocks drops the pan on the counter and pinches the bridge of his nose. "No, T. No." He spins and braces his hands on the countertop at his sides. "I would have preferred if you had listened to me when I said we were leaving, or at least your best friend. We were having a good day and your rebellious streak got the best of you, once again. You just had to go and ride with someone you don't know, in an event you've never done, and this is the outcome."

"So, you want to control me? Is that it? You put this ring on my finger and want me to be an obedient bitch?"

"Don't start putting words into my mouth. I want you to give a damn about your wellbeing. I fucking love you and only want what is best for you! But watching you be that reckless today, with zero regard for yourself while me, your best friend, and your brother begged you not to do it—you ignored all of us. Do you love me, T? Really? Or do you enjoy pushing my feelings aside and treating me like my opinions and I don't matter?"

Tonya slowly stands, her features are unreadable. She stares at the cowboy standing in her kitchen, his green eyes full of something she's never seem him show her before.

He's unsure.

"Hocks," she whispers, her chest feeling as if it's breaking at the mere thought of what he is insinuating.

"Answer me, T. Do you love me or is this all some fun game? I thought I knew. I thought things would change and you would take better care of keeping yourself safe. I watched you—" his voice cracks, and he drops his chin. "I've watched you for the past four years without the right to step in or say anything, but that ring on your finger means I now have a right, and we're getting this squared away before what happened today happens again."

Tears well in her eyes, and she steps around the couch. "Of course, I love you. How could you ask me that? You're the only person I've let in since—" She shakes her head. Her past comes rushing to the forefront of her mind and she steels herself. Taking a step back, she lifts her gaze to her fiancé. "What are you going to do? Leave again? It was so easy for you last time."

Hocks strides across the room and snatches her hand, placing it on his chest. "Don't. We aren't throwing things in each other's faces like teenagers. We're going to have a conversation like two adults. You want to ski? Fine, but we're setting up a course and practicing. I'll buy you skis. I'll be the rider and your partner because I don't trust another soul with your life. Darlin', I am not controlling you. This is how a relationship works. We're partners and we make decisions together. First one being, your life is more important than acting like a brat."

Tonya's cheeks flush and she tries to pull her hand away. "Let go of me."

"No. Because you aren't running away and I'm not running away. Not unless you tell me you want me to leave. But you better be damn sure because I'm not making a habit of having this same conversation. I love you. I want to marry you. You're the most important person to me in my life, T. Do you want me?"

His green eyes shine as he gazes down at her. His hand trembles atop hers on his chest, terrified that he has pushed her too far. Slowly her enraged blue eyes soften until she resembles the woman who let down her walls at the cabin under the northern lights.

"Tonya Faye," he says, his voice softer, and he angles her chin up. "Do you want me to leave?"

"No!" she cries out, tears escaping and cascading down her cheeks. "I don't know how to do this." She waves a hand between them. "I didn't mean to hurt your feelings today or scare you. What I did today is exactly what I would've done last year when—"

"When you were single and looking for an adrenaline high," he supplies, and her bottom lip quivers.

"I'm sorry. I do love you. I don't want you to leave. Not ever."

"Oh, darlin'," Hocks coos, wrapping her in his arms and pulling her close. His chin rests atop her head, and she buries her nose into his chest. "I'm not going anywhere. Never again, not as long as you'll have me and want me. You don't have to worry about that, T. But I can't live with this curdling fear in my stomach every time I disagree with you. I'm sorry too. I'm sorry I let it get this far before talking to you about it."

He kisses her hair and she clings to his jacket.

"I love you, Stud."

Hocks smirks and rests his cheek on her head. "I love you, darlin'. Go take a shower and I'll fix us dinner, okay?"

She nods and sniffles, her red-rimmed, puffy eyes nearly break Hocks' heart. Kissing her lips softly, he brushes his thumbs across her cheeks, wiping away her tears.

"I'm glad that's settled." He smiles, and she refrains from rolling her eyes.

"Very few people get to see me cry. Just remember that." A smirk plays on her lips and he relaxes, knowing that he still has her.

Chapter Thirteen

By the time Hocks has the thrown together dinner fixed and on the table, Tonya comes out of the bedroom in her bathrobe and face free of makeup. This is the side of her that is his favorite. The woman who is completely unmasked and baring every part of herself to him. He smiles. Earlier's argument is already forgotten.

"Breakfast?" she asks, and he grins.

"We know my cooking skills are far from amazing. I figured pancakes, bacon, and eggs would work."

She blushes, an odd sense of shyness creeping across her cheeks and Hocks wonders if the conversation earlier did more than make her realize how much she hurt him today. She's acting like she did the first time her parents invited him over for dinner. He sits across from her and studies her movements while he pours syrup over his plate.

When she catches him staring, she quickly looks away and shoves a bite of eggs into her mouth.

In silence, they eat, the scraping of forks and sounds of them swallowing is all that converses between them.

"T," Hocks starts when he can't take it anymore. "You seem...broken?" he says, not sure how else to describe it.

"Broken how?"

"Like we've reverted to this place where you don't know how to act around me. What is it? Was it earlier? If there is something else you need to say, get it off your chest and let's hash it out. Anything is better than this."

Abruptly, she stands and Hocks moves to go after her. Before he reaches the bedroom door, she comes back out, holding a wrapped box with a bow on it.

"What's this?" he asks, hesitantly reaching for the box.

"Your Christmas present—well, one of them."

"But Christmas is tomorrow." The box is light, like it barely contains anything.

"I need you to open this one tonight," she whispers, her tone nearly pleading. He walks to the couch and sits, ripping the paper from the box and opening it.

It's empty, minus a tag, and he lifts it, flipping it in his fingers. "What is—"

His words are cut off as Tonya's robe falls to the floor. Her breasts are covered by a bright red bow with a matching thong and bright red stockings up to her mid-thighs.

Hocks' mouth goes dry, and he stares at the woman before him.

"I want you, Stud. Today, tomorrow, for the rest of my life, and I never want to make you doubt that. I love you, Hocks."

He tosses the box to the floor and rushes toward Tonya, but she holds up a finger and stops him, a gleam sparkling in her eyes.

He watches her walk to the table where their dishes sit, and she picks up the syrup bottle. Holding it to her sternum, she gently squeezes the bottle until a small stream of syrup drips down her chest and between her breasts.

"Oops," she says, pouting her bottom lip and giving Hocks a daring glare.

He shoves his hat off his head, his cock springing to attention against his zipper, and closes the distance between them. Wrapping his arms around her waist, her back bows and his needy tongue plunges between her breasts, licking up the sweet taste of the syrup. Tonya giggles and her head falls back at the attention.

Hocks licks, bites, and sucks across her collarbone and up her throat until he reaches her lips. Plunging his tongue between her lips, he steals her breath as his mouth ravishes her like she's made of the sweet nectar.

She's never had someone speak about how they care about her like Hocks. Any other man would have walked out the moment she tried to shut down earlier, but not him. Not her fiancé. He's proved time and time again that he's in this for the long haul and he's right. She needs to live her life differently than the woman she was with no happy ending in sight.

Her fingers weave through his long hair. He keeps meaning to get it cut, but honestly, she likes the way she can grab it. His hands move down to cup her ass, and he lifts her to wrap her legs around his waist.

"This is the perfect Christmas present, darlin'." He lays her back on the bed and she tugs on the bow covering her chest. It comes undone, exposing her breast while she still wears the bra. "Fucking hell, T." Hocks groans, ripping his shirt, then pants and briefs off.

"Show me what happens when I don't listen to you, Stud. Remind me of who I belong to." Tonya dips a hand between her thighs.

Hocks grabs her knees and pushes them to the side, exposing her red lace-covered pussy. "All of this," he says, running a finger from her ankle to her clit. "Is staying on." Hungrily, he crawls across the mattress and grabs a pillow to shove under her ass. With one hand, he pushes her thong to the side and drags his tongue from her center to her clit. Tonya sucks in a breath as Hocks sucks and bites on her sensitive bundle of nerves.

He doesn't go slow. He builds her up so quickly once her orgasm hits, she nearly blacks out and forgets how to breathe. Her legs shake as her pussy clenches around nothing.

"Hocks," she mewls, as he continues his assault even after her vision comes back into focus. Every touch of his nose, his scruffy beard, and tongue are like tiny zaps of electricity to her center.

"Who do you belong to, darlin'? Say it," he breathes against her skin and dips his tongue into her creamy center.

"You. Fuck!" she cries out. "You! I belong to you, now *please*," she drags the word *please* with a guttural plea. "Get inside of me."

"That's right, T. You are mine and you're going to take my cock like the good fucking girl you are. Just for me."

Tonya's mouth falls open at his words, and he drags her ass to the edge of the bed and buries himself inside of her. Skin slaps against skin as he thrusts into her repeatedly, her soft cries of pleasure egging him on.

When his muscles tighten and he grips her hips to pull her snuggly against his pelvis, his cock jerks.

"My fucking girl," he groans, bracing himself over her body and tucking her hair behind her ear.

She playfully bites his thumb, and he knows without a doubt, this will be the best Christmas ever.

Chapter Fourteen

Connor rolls over in the bed, his arm reaching for Marni, but he's met with cold, empty space. He sits up in the bed and glances around the empty bedroom.

"Mar?" he calls out, jerking the blankets back and walking into the living area where the fire in the stove has been recently tended to. Wearing nothing but his briefs, he checks the kitchen and finds a note on the table.

Gone to run an errand. I'll be back before you know it.

-Mar

Connor thumps his fist on the counter. He hoped, since this was their first Christmas, he'd wake up to his fiancé. Turns out there is someone who is more of an early riser than he is. Glancing at the clock, he decides to start his day. Marni has a little less than three hours before she's due to be back, and he's going to count down to the minute to make sure she is.

He sends her a quick text, then gets dressed and starts a pot of coffee. A few minutes later, his phone chimes and he smiles at her, telling him Merry Christmas.

It would have been better if I could have had sex with my fiancé this morning.

When he checks his phone as he climbs in the truck, he notices her response.

It'll be worth it. I promise.

I doubt it; he thinks to himself. Nothing tops how she feels to him.

When he reaches the barn, the lights are all out and the horses stir with soft snorts and whinnies.

"You know, living with your sister has its perks," Hocks announces as he strolls in.

"Don't—" Connor warns.

"I don't have to worry about you firing me for being late to work." Hocks shoves his best friend's shoulder.

"We're still paying you, so technically I could fire you and then you'd still have to work for free."

Hocks shakes his head and points at the horses.

"Touche. Let's feed these guys real quick. I have to go get Tonya's present before she wakes up—which by how late I had her up last night—" He wiggles his eyebrows and Connor walks away. "Come on, man! You make this so easy!"

***

Marni makes it back to the ranch and with Stacy and Jack's help, Connor is inside with his head under a *leaky sink* where he won't be able to see what her errand was.

She steps inside the farmhouse right on time and inhales the smell of the Christmas meal Stacy has been working on since before sunrise.

"Where did you say there was water? I don't see anything?" Connor's muffled shouts come from the kitchen and Marni rolls her lips between her teeth to hide her smile.

When she steps through the kitchen door, Stacy beams at her, then turns to Connor.

"Maybe I was imagining it. These eyes aren't what they used to be."

He sighs and takes two deep breaths before shimmying himself free from the cabinet. His gaze catches on Marni leaning in the doorway and he immediately smiles.

"Early morning errands?" he asks, narrowing his gaze, but her features give nothing away. She walks over and offers her hand to help him off the floor.

"Merry Christmas, my future husband." She reaches up to her tip-toes and gives him a quick kiss. He takes a deep breath and brushes his thumb along her jaw.

"Do you want to go home for a bit?" His gaze holds the promise of everything he wanted to do this morning.

Home. She still isn't used to Connor calling his cabin their home. "I'd love to...but,"

"But?" he asks, stepping in closer to her.

Jack clears his throat and Stacy slaps his shoulder. Connor drops his chin and grabs his cowboy hat from the counter, placing it back on his head.

"I was going to help your mom with the food," Marni adds, giving his hand a squeeze and moving further into the kitchen beside Stacy. Jack chuckles and places a hand on Connor's shoulder.

"And you can help me fill the firewood bin on the porch."

"Of course," Connor says, stealing one last glance at Marni before following his dad outside.

Once he and Jack are out of the house, Stacy leans in close to Marni. "So, did you get it?" she asks, her voice full of excitement.

Marni nods and nearly bounces on her toes. "I did! I just hope it makes him happy and not somehow worse."

Stacy wraps her in a side hug and rubs her hand up and down Marni's arm. "I think the gift is perfect and you have nothing to worry about."

"Thank you...for your help today."

"Of course! It was fun being all secretive. Now," Stacy adds, bracing herself on the counter. "How bad was it with Tonya yesterday?"

Marni's eyes widen and her cheeks heat. "Yesterday?"

Stacy narrows her gaze. "Susan called. And I already know there was an ER visit. I'll be sure to throttle her for that later."

Marni laughs, but it comes out breathy. As long as Tonya doesn't think her best friend is the one who told her mother, they'll be good.

Chapter Fifteen

THE TABLE IS SET and Stacy puts the finishing touches on her meal by the time Tonya and Hocks walk in.

"Well, look who it is," Stacy teases. "Bout time you find your way up here. Marni and Connor helped get things ready, so you two are in charge of cleanup."

Hocks drops his chin and Tonya smiles wide at her mother. "Wouldn't be Christmas any other way."

Stacy kisses her forehead as she walks past, and everyone takes their seats around the table.

"There's also a talk to be had about yesterday," Stacy chastises, and Tonya immediately looks at Marni.

Her best friend rases her arms in innocence, and Stacy shakes her head.

"Marni didn't rat you out, but this is a small town, dear."

Tonya groans and leans back in her seat. "You really don't have to. I learned my lesson and I promise I'll be more careful from now on."

Connor's fork sits suspended from shoveling honey ham into his plate. He looks at his best friend, who has a proud smile.

He actually got to her. He really is the best damn thing to happen to his sister and all the ill feelings he's had since yesterday melt away. Tonya doesn't say something like that light-heartedly. She meant it. She's going to be more careful and finally grow up.

"Well," Stacy says, holding her hands out to her side. "I guess it's time to bless the food, then."

Dinner is full of laughs with secretive smiles as the anticipation of giving gifts grows closer. Everyone steals secret glances at one another between bites of the delicious family meal.

Jack places his hand over his wife's beside him on the table. Her cheeks blush and she glances at him, her gray eyes full of everything she isn't saying.

Turning her hand over, she squeezes her husband's and thinks about everything they've overcome to get here. Their dreams came true. Their table is full with their children and the ones who love them as much as they do.

Once the meal is done, Tonya and Hocks wash the empty plates and glasses, covering the left overs for when supper rolls around and everyone gets hungry again.

"Okay, present time!" Stacy says, clapping her hands together. Marni and Connor curl up on the love seat while Stacy and Jack snuggle in the recliner.

"My turn!" Tonya exclaims, surprising everyone with her enthusiasm. She grabs a box from under the tree and hands it to Hocks, vibrating with excitement as he chuckles at her display. They sit side by side on the floor and Hocks shifts as all eyes land on him.

"I'll be right back," Connor murmurs into Marni's ear, kissing her before he gets up.

Hocks rips through the paper and opens a box to a brand new felt Stetson. He picks it up and his eyes widen in shock.

"There's more," she says, turning it over in his hands. On the underside of the rim, Curston is burned into the felt.

His eyes sting, and he swallows the lump in his throat. "T," he says, unsure of how to convey what this gift means to him.

"You're a Curston," she says, placing her hand on his leg.

"She's right," Jack adds, and Stacy nods, her eyes misting over.

Hocks clears his throat and removes his hat, placing his new one on his head. "How does it look?" he asks.

"Perfect." Tonya beams.

"Okay, your turn," he says. "But you'll need your jacket and your boots." He pushes up to his feet and Tonya looks around the room.

"What is it?"

Hocks holds his hand out to her. "You'll just have to trust me."

Connor steps back into the living room in time to see everyone moving. "What's going on?" he asks.

"Tonya's gift is outside, it seems," Marni says with a smile.

Hocks leads them to a trailer parked behind the barn hooked up to his truck. The door creaks as it swings open and Tonya steps around to look inside.

Her hands fly to her mouth and she squeals. "You didn't! Oh, my goodness!"

Marni can't help her curiosity and steps up beside her. "Awh! Look how cute!"

Standing in the trailer is a shaggy light brown cow with its horns askew, one turned down while the other is turned up.

"It was at the sale a month ago and the Callahans have been nice enough to keep him for me. For obvious reasons, nobody wanted him because he didn't fit the normal look of the highland cows."

Tonya barely hears what Hocks says as she climbs into the trailer. "Hey buddy, you never have to worry about being unwanted again. You'll fit right in with the misfits, won't you?"

He sniffs her hand and lets her pet his forehead.

Marni walks over to Connor, who wears an exasperated expression. "Be happy for her. It's simply adorable."

"She's turning this place into a petting zoo," he grumbles, and Marni nudges her grumpy cowboy.

"Since we're outside, I think it's your turn." Marni takes his hand and leads him toward the barn. Tonya backs out of the trailer and follows her best friend and brother along with Hocks, Stacy and Jack.

Connor tightens his grip as they walk into the barn. "Close your eyes," Marni orders, and he does as she asks.

She leads him through the barn to the very last stall at the farm back and everyone gasps behind him.

"What?" he opens his eyes, and he's facing a stall with a bay yearling horse inside. He steps closer to the filly that resembles so much of Brimstone. Opening the latch, he steps inside and the young horse sniffs his outstretched hand.

The rest of the family stands outside the stall. Stacy's hands are clutched to her chest as her son greets the filly.

"Her grandparents on the dam's side were Brimstone's parents," Marni whispers, worried about telling him that tidbit of information.

Connor smiles and runs his hand down the horse's neck and back.

"She's beautiful," he whispers and glances at his fiancé across the gate. "She's perfect." He carefully closes the gate and wraps his arms around Marni, spinning her in the middle of the barn aisle.

She giggles and hangs on until he sets her down. "Makes my gift feel way less significant."

"It's not a competition, Connor. I'm sure it'll be perfect."

He leads her to the tack room at the front of the barn and tells her to close her eyes. She bounces on giddy toes as he rolls the door open and moves to stand beside her.

"Ready?"

"Mhmm!"

Her eyes spring open. Inside the tack stall on a saddle stand, sits a new leather saddle with Orion's name engraved on the cannel and a new bridle with a leather halter hanging on the horn. Marni walks closer and runs her hand over the leather and lifts the halter to find Orion engraved in a metal plate on the cheeks.

"I took your saddle to show wear of it to match the fit to your seat. I figured since you're riding down the aisle, Orion required a new outfit, too." Connor steps up behind her, running his hands across her shoulders. "Do you like it?"

She spins in his hands and grips his jacket. "This is real," she says with tears in her eyes. Stacy nudges Hocks and Tonya to give them some privacy and they walk back outside to see her new highland cow.

"What's real?" Connor says, not following.

"You. Me. Us. This." She lifts her ring finger and shows off her engagement ring. "Somehow, my life has turned around and I'm getting everything I've ever wanted. Sometimes it still seems surreal."

Connor cups her cheek and mashes his lips to hers, desperate to push down any doubt that this is her life and it's all real.

"You're where you've always belonged, Mar," he says, his hat sliding back as he presses his forehead to hers.

"Just took me a few left turns to get here," she teases. "And in three weeks, it'll be official." She lays her cheek on his coat and sighs.

"I'm sorry your parents didn't show up," he says, knowing that even though it isn't something Marni talks about, it bothers her.

"I can't say I expected them to. I hoped, but that always leads to disappointment."

Connor hugs her tighter, hoping that her parents will make an effort to show up to the wedding at least. Marni deserves so much more than their bare minimum, but he knows it would mean the world to her if they did.

Chapter Sixteen

Marni watches Connor as he whispers sweet things to his new yearling. "Keep talking to her like that and I might get jealous," she teases.

Connor scoffs and scratches around the filly's ears.

"I have one favor," he says, catching Marni off guard.

"What is it?" she asks.

"Will you train her like you did Brimstone? She was the best." His voice grows thick and Marni nods.

"Of course, and I can teach you how to do it yourself. You'll be a better team for it. It will be fun." She opens the stall door and stands with her hand on her hip. "But for now, we have to go give your parents their gifts. Hocks and Tonya just got back from taking her new little guy to meet its fellow misfits."

"I'm going to deck Hocks for adding another ridiculous animal to this ranch."

Marni loops her arm through his. "Don't be such a grump. If it makes her happy, who are you to stand in her way?"

He rolls his eyes and kisses the crown of her head. "I'm not a grump."

She pinches her fingers close together and squints. "You're a bit of a grump."

He moves his hand to tickle her ribs, and she takes off running in a fit of laughter to the house.

Inside Tonya and Hocks fix a plate of leftovers and put them in the microwave when Marni bursts through the back door, followed by a laughing Connor.

Marni slides to a stop, and Conner nearly collides into her. "Hey! Are we ready?" she asks and Tonya nods.

"They're in the living room." She and Hocks set their plates down before going to find her parents.

Jack and Stacy sit side-by-side on the love seat and glance up as their children walk in. Not just Connor and Tonya, but they consider Hocks and Marni as their children, too.

"There's one more gift to give," Tonya announces, reaching behind the Christmas tree and pulling out an envelope.

Stacy sits straighter and Jack picks up his reading glasses from the table.

"You guys didn't have to get us anything. We have everything we need right here."

The four stand in a line as Tonya fidgets with the paper between her fingers. "You guys have told us your wedding story more times than I can count. You built this house, the barn, the entire ranch from nothing. You two are an inspiration."

Jack places his hand on Stacy's leg and smiles proudly.

"But there was one thing you never mentioned," Connor says. "Something we think you two deserve and will really enjoy."

Tonya hands Stacy the envelope and she opens it. She quickly reads the printed document and glances from the paper to her children, then back again. "What is this?"

Jack sits straighter and reads over his wife's shoulder.

Tonya takes Hocks' hand, and she smirks. "It's your honeymoon. All expenses paid. Food, housing, and plane tickets. The whole thing while you travel through Europe for ten days. It isn't until May when the weather will be nicer."

"And you'll need passports," Connor adds.

Stacy's mouth falls open. She's never dreamed she and Jack would travel out of the country. "We're really going to Paris, Italy, London, and Spain?"

Jack rubs a hand down her back and leans forward. "This ole cowboy is going to Europe." He shakes his head in disbelief.

Stacy pushes to her feet and wraps all four of her children in a bone-crushing hug. "You guys! This is so much! Too much," she says with a shaky voice.

"There is one more thing," Marni adds, and Stacy pulls back.

All eyes turn to her and she pulls out three identical boxes from under the couch.

"You didn't have to get us anything," Tonya chastises, but Marni insists.

Connor eyes her warily and takes the box she hands to him. Giving one to her best friend and her fiancé, then Stacy and Jack.

"Okay, open them," she says, stepping back with sweating palms.

Simultaneously, they rip the wrapping paper and are met with a white box. Popping the tape, they remove the lid and Marni's heart falls into her stomach as she waits.

"What?" Tonya squeals at the same time Stacy shrieks. They each hold up an onesie outfit, announcing there will be a baby Curston coming in August. Connor stares at his opened box, his bright blue eyes brimming with tears as his fingers run across the laid out onesie.

"There's more," Marni whispers, and Connor looks up, barely holding back his emotions. They all dig deeper into the box and the room goes silent. Underneath the tissue paper is another onesie, with the words *not just one, but two are due*.

Marni places her hands over her stomach as Connor tosses his box aside and grabs his future wife.

"I'm going to be a dad?" he asks, his voice shaking and Marni can't hold it together. She chokes out a sob and buries her face into his shoulder.

"Yes."

"We're getting twins! I'm going to be an aunt!" Tonya shouts and hugs Stacy.

Connor leans back, his blue eyes shining with unshed tears and he gets lost in the chocolate brown eyes that have always captivated him. If his babies get her eyes, he'll never be able to tell them no.

"Are you happy?" she asks him.

"I'm beyond happy, Mar. You've given me more than I ever thought I'd have." He places his hand on her stomach and smiles. "You're going to be a fantastic mother and these two don't stand a chance with Mom and Dad. You know that, right?"

She nods and places her hand over his. "We're going to have a family."

Connor laughs and kisses her forehead. "Is this why you didn't want to wait until spring to get married?"

"I suspected," she says with a soft smile.

Jack claps Connor on the shoulder and pulls his son in for a hug. Joy-filled tears fall down Stacy's cheeks as she wraps her arms around Marni.

"This is better than any present," she cheers.

They love Marni as if she was their own, and it shows. Marni glances at the couch where a fourth box sits, unopened.

Family isn't defined by blood and she's reminded of that time and time again. The people on this ranch are her family.

Chapter Seventeen

Connor lays his head on Marni's stomach in their bed and she runs her fingers through her hair.

"Do you think they can hear me?" he asks, his voice thick with sleep at the early morning hour.

She chuckles, and he pushes himself up the bed to run his hands over her hair.

"Are you laughing at me?" he asks, his gaze more than a little mischievous. He drops his head to tickle her ribs and her giggles morph into hysterical laughter.

"No! No!" she squeals between breaths.

He relents and kisses her lips before standing from the bed. "In two days, you'll be Mrs. Marni Curston."

She pushes up to her elbows and runs through a mental list of everything they need to prepare for the wedding at the ranch. The ceremony will be inside the barn, however, she and Tonya are going to ride up to the barn instead of walking down an aisle. Then they'll move inside the farmhouse for the reception.

It'll be small, twenty to thirty people at most. Marni's parents swear they're coming, but Connor can't help but worry they'll let their daughter down again.

Her brown eyes get this faraway look and Connor leans down, cupping her cheek. "Hey, where'd you go?"

"Just a lot to get through in two days."

"It'll be fine." His phone rings and Marni flings the quilts back. The to-do list isn't going to finish itself.

Across the ranch, Tonya and Hocks stand in the middle of the misfits with the sunrise.

"Have you decided on a name yet?" Hocks asks as the new highland cow sniffs Reginald, the miniature pony, through the fence.

"I think I'm going to go with Hamish," Tonya smirks.

"Hamish?" Hocks questions with a chuckle.

"Yes, he looks like a Hamish."

Reginald snorts and Foxy, the goose, honks at the sudden sound.

"How long are you going to keep them separated?"

"A few more days. Give them time to get used to each other first. Daisy and Mandy haven't shown much interest yet, and I don't want him hurting them." She points at the pot-belly pig and goat hiding inside the shed.

"I think they just don't like the snow," Hocks remarks, taking a long drink of his coffee.

Tonya's phone rings and she bites her glove to pull it off her hand to answer.

"What's up?" she asks her brother on the other end.

Hocks' notices the shift in her stance and Tonya turns to gaze in the direction of the farmhouse.

"Okay, we'll be right there."

She hangs up and takes a deep breath.

"We need to go to the farmhouse. Now."

Connor and Marni drive by as Hocks and Tonya get into their truck. They're all walking into the farmhouse together to find Stacy crying in the kitchen.

"Mom?" Tonya asks while Connor walks deeper into the house.

"It's ruined. It's all ruined," she whimpers. "I'm so sorry, girls."

Connor finds Jack on his knees in the living room, running a tired hand over his head. Water stands in the far corner of the room and all the furniture has been moved to where the water hasn't reached.

"How bad?" Connor asks.

Jack pushes to his feet, his shoulders sagging. "It's the whole back of the house. Bathroom, kitchen, guest room. It started in here, but we caught it when we woke up this morning. I shut off the water and you see the rest."

There's no way they can have the wedding here now. It's too cold to have both the reception and ceremony outside or even in the barn.

His excitement fades into dread. He has to confirm his fiancé's fears that they won't be getting married this weekend.

Marni steps into the living room threshold. Her expression has Connor waving for her to come closer.

"I'm sorry, baby," Connor whispers into her ear, and she pulls back, giving him a small smile.

"It's fine. We'll just wait. I have to call the florist and eat the cost with it being this close. Then call Mom and Dad and everyone else that was supposed to come."

Hocks and Tonya steps into the doorway, Tonya wearing a similar expression as Marni. "I'll help you," she says to her best friend.

Marni nods and leaves the living room to make her list of calls.

Taking a steadying breath to hold back the tears, she calls the florist, trying not to think about the amount of money this is costing them.

"Dreaming of Dahlias. How can we help you?" Carly, the employee, answers.

"Hi, I need to speak with Dahlia please," Marni says.

There's a shuffle from the other end of the line and Marni chews on her lip while Tonya helps Stacy soak up the water on the kitchen floor.

"This is Dahlia," the business owner says.

"Hello, this is Marni Foster," Marni responds.

"Hey, is everything okay? I was finishing up your bouquet, actually."

Marni blinks back the tears and rolls her lips between her teeth. Pressing her hand to her forehead, she swallows the lump in her throat. She feels ridiculous having this reaction to postponing the wedding. It doesn't change anything. She still has Connor, her babies, and her home. Yet, she can't help the feeling of a total loss breaking her heart.

"Hello?" Dahlia asks and Marni shakes her head and promises to let herself feel all these emotions later.

"Sorry, I'm here. We hit a snag this morning on the ranch. The farmhouse had a waterline freeze and bust... We are going to have to postpone the wedding. I'm sorry. I know there's no way we could find another venue this short of notice and I understand if you can't refund it. It is what it is."

"Wait," Dahlia says, and Marni's brows furrow. "If we found another venue that wasn't the ranch, would you still want to go through with it?"

She looks at her best friend and Tonya mouths, '*What is it*'.

"I'd have to talk to Tonya, Connor, and Hocks, but what can you find two days before?" Hope rises in her chest again. As much as the ranch means to them, marrying the man she loves beside her best friend this weekend makes the location seem irrelevant.

"You find out if they'd be on board and I'll make some calls," Dahlia tells her and hangs up the phone.

Tonya stands and Marni stares at her phone. "What did she say?"

"She wants to know if we would be okay with using a different venue—if she can find one this short of notice. I told her I had to ask you all first."

Connor and Hocks step inside the kitchen. They glance from Tonya to Marni with raised eyebrows in question.

"If it means I get to marry Hocks this weekend, then yes. I'm on board," Tonya says.

"On board with what?" Connor asks, looking at Marni.

"That was the wedding florist who seems to think she can find us a wedding venue for this weekend. But we all have to agree. I know what this ranch means to you, and I understand if you want to wait."

He shakes his head and walks to her, cupping her cheeks with both hands. "I want to marry you. I want you to have the wedding you want."

Marni nods. "And what about your parents?"

"Oh sweetie," Stacy says, and they all turn to look at her and Jack as they walk in. "The place isn't what's important. It's the people there to celebrate with us. We say yes. Call Dahlia and see if we get to watch you two walk down the aisle this weekend."

Marni glances at each of their faces. She's met with confidence from each person and the defeat she was feeling earlier morphs into hope once again.

The phone rings once.

"Dreaming of Dahlias," Dahlia answers.

"It's Marni Foster calling you back. If you can find us another venue, we'll take it."

"Actually, I found one. Haynes Venues has a barn and a cabin both open this weekend."

Chapter Eighteen

MARNI AND TONYA SIT back-to-back in what would be the master bedroom except it's set up for the bridal party before the weddings.

"Are you ready?" Tonya asks, giddiness filling her high-pitched voice.

"Yes...are you?" her best friend responds, fidgeting with her hands at her front. Susan and Stacy stand off to the side, their eyes shining as they wait for the two women to turn and give each other the first looks.

"1," Tonya says.

"2," Marni continues.

"3," they say in unison and spin.

Marni's hair cascades down around her shoulders in soft, silky waves. Her brown eyes pop against the natural makeup, dusting her features, and she covers her mouth as she takes in her beautiful best friend.

"T," she says, admiring the half up-do, with a braid around the crown. Her makeup is slightly more dramatic, but doesn't take away from the simplicity of her beige wedding dress, with lace decorating the front and tapering off around her ankles. Where Tonya's dress has a plunging neckline, Marni's is more reserved with a goddess neckline and flowing out at her waist.

"We look fucking amazing!" T shrieks and Marni laughs at her best friend's choice of words.

"Tonya Faeye," Stacy chastises and sniffles, dabbing her eyes to keep from smearing her makeup.

"C'mon Stace, she ain't wrong." Susan grins and crosses her arms. "You two are simply beautiful. These men won't know what hit them.

There's a soft knock on the door and Stacy cracks it. "Marni?" she says, and pulls the door open further. Gwen stands on the other side of the door frame wearing a soft purple dress and her hair styled in a curly bun on her head.

"Mom?" Marni says, wondering if she's seeing things.

"Hey, honey. Sorry we're late. Your dad got lost and wouldn't stop to ask for directions."

Marni forgets about every wrongdoing her mother has done and gathers the bottom of her dress, walks across the room and pulls Gwen into a hug. "I'm so glad you came," she whispers, and notices how her mother stiffens, then relaxes before embracing her in return.

"We wouldn't have missed this," Gwen says, placing her hands on Marni's shoulders and stepping back to take in her daughter. "We're so sorry about the ranch and as our wedding present, your father and I want to pay for this venue. It's the least we can do for our daughter."

Marni stares, shocked at her mother's offer. "That's incredibly sweet, but—"

"She means, thank you," Tonya says, cutting off her.

Stacy steps forward holding a plastic case with a mother of the bride corsage inside. "Here, you'll need this."

Gwen takes the case and hovers her hand over the simple white lilies.

"Okay, we have dads to show our dresses to," Tonya says, clapping her hands together. She takes Stacy's arm and Gwen offers hers to Marni as they walk out of the bridal room. Susan hurries ahead of them and orders the dads to face away and ensures the men upstairs don't sneak out to take a peek.

Stacy and Gwen move to stand beside their husbands and tell them to turn around.

Jack wipes at his eyes, and his face turns red as he tries to hold back the tears. Tonya hasn't let anything get to her yet today, but seeing her father cry has a lump forming in her throat and she embraces him, feeling like a little girl.

Gerald stares at Marni with soft eyes, his lips pursed in a saddened smile.

"Dad?" she asks, acutely aware of Tonya embracing Jack beside her.

His lips part, but no sound comes out. Lifting his hands with his palms up, he shudders out a breath. "You look beautiful, Marni. Truly." Opening his arms wider, Marni steps forward and Gerald wraps his arms around her.

Today feels like a dream for Marni. Not only is she marrying a man who loves her, but both her parents are here and are genuinely happy for her.

"Thank you," Marni responds and steps back, tilting her head to keep the tears at bay.

"Marni," her best friend says, and she glances over at her. Tonya places her hands on her stomach and jerks her chin toward Gwen and Gerald.

Oh, right. Marni clears her throat and faces her parents. She hadn't told them because she clung to the hope she would see them today and could tell them in person.

"Mom, Dad," she says, gaining the attention of everyone in the room. "I have something to tell you guys. Connor and I are expecting our first babies in August."

In slow motion, she watches her mother's features go from confused to shocked. Then something Marni has only seen Gwen Foster wear a few times. She imagines it's how all parents look at their children with love and overwhelmed emotions, but for Marni it is foreign.

Gwen squeals and fists both hands in front of her mouth. Marni stumbles back. She's never seen her mother show excitement over anything, and she's not sure if it's good or bad.

Chapter Nineteen

HOCKS PACES THE FLOOR in the upstairs bedroom where he and Connor have been ordered to stay until they're told otherwise.

"We're going to have to pay extra for the path you're wearing on the carpet," Connor jokes as he kicks back in the recliner.

"How are you so calm? Where are your wedding jitters and nerves?"

"I've been waiting for this day since I was twenty years old and I knew I loved that girl downstairs. The only emotion I'm feeling is impatient, but I know how to control it."

Hocks scoffs and continues pacing. "Easy for you to say. You have so much to offer Marni and-and she loves you. You basically saved her from her shit life and all I got Tonya was held at gunpoint."

Connor's brows furrow, and he pushes to his feet. "Hey, man. My sister loves you and that's all that matters. You've practically been a part of this family since we hired you. Now you'll be official."

"I love the shit out of her," Hocks says, smiling widely as he pictures his fiancé's face.

"That's obvious."

Screams erupt from downstairs and Connor grabs the doorknob, already turning it with Hocks right on his heels. The door crashes open and Susan ushers Marni and Tonya back just as Connor and Hocks look over the upstairs balcony.

"What are you doing?" Susan snaps. "You're supposed to stay in your room."

Connor ignores her and balks at the sight of Gerald and Gwen, both with tears misting their eyes. He leans over the railing, searching for his woman among the chaos.

"I'm fine," Marni shouts and even though he can't see her, he knows by the tone of her voice it's true.

Susan rolls her eyes. "She was simply telling her parents the good news about your babies."

Gwen's mouth hangs open like a fish. "Two," she murmurs and Gerald's grin widens.

Connor nods.

"You good, darlin'?" Hocks shouts out.

"Yes. Ready to marry your ass," she responds.

"Me too."

Susan huffs and waves at the two grooms. "Nobody will be marrying anyone's asses if you don't get back into your rooms. We have—" She flips the watch on her wrist. "Actually, girls, you go back. It's time to take the men to the barn. Our guests are arriving and it's nearly show time."

"I love you!" Marni shouts, and Connor grins.

"I'll see you at the altar!"

"We don't have an altar. We're in a barn," Tonya shouts back and Hocks laughs.

"Okay, that's enough of that," Susan reprimands.

"Grown adults and they still act like children," Jack teases and Stacy leans her head on his shoulder.

"I hope they never stop," she muses, and Jack kisses her temple.

"Okay! Grooms, I need you down here and ready! Hocks, fix your tie! Parents, if you want to come with me, we'll get you situated in the lineup and then I'll come back for the brides after the grooms are front and center." Everyone reacts to Susan's orders and takes their places.

Hocks and Connor pause outside the hallway downstairs that leads to the bridal room. Hocks slaps his best friend on the back and grins.

"Ready to get hitched? Get the ole ball and chain until death do us part?"

Connor shoves him off and straightens his cowboy hat. "You are ridiculous."

Inside the barn, the small gathering of family and friends takes their seats. The tables are pushed to the sides and back of the open space. White daylilies decorate the aisle chairs and arch at the front of the room.

Susan straightens Hocks' tie and opens the door for them to walk down the aisle and take their place. She closes the door to a crack and once the grooms are in place; she ushers the Fosters down the aisle. Stacy stands with Tonya's wedding bouquet of white daylilies. Susan holds a similar one for Marni.

She angles her head to look up at her husband. His hair is gray from the years they've spent together and permanent laugh lines wrinkle his eyes and mouth.

"Hm?" she says when his blue eyes search her face for a response to a question she didn't hear.

"Are you okay, Stace?"

Jack places a hand on the small of her back.

"I got stuck in a memory. A really good memory," she admits and her eyes sparkle with the love and adoration thirty years have brought them.

"Which one would that be?" he asks, a smile teasing his lips.

"The day we met."

"Ah. Was it really good? I vaguely remember someone wanted nothing to do with me." He chuckles and kisses her forehead. He crooks his elbow out to her and Stacy slips her hand over his forearm. "Are you ready to see our girls before they walk down the aisle?"

Stacy smiles so wide her cheeks ache, and she grips her daughter's wedding bouquet.

“We did it, Jack. Can you believe it? Both our babies found their soulmates.”

Jack places his hand over hers on his arm and squeezes. “I never doubted us, sweetheart.”

Chapter Twenty

"ARE YOU READY TO be my sister?" Tonya asks, beaming at Marni, her best friend since they were kids.

"Absolutely."

They take their bouquets from Susan and Stacy before the Curstons disappear behind the cracked door.

"Who would have ever thought we'd end up here, best friends marrying best friends," Marni remarks.

"Okay girls, you ready?" Susan asks.

They nod and hook elbows with each other. "I would have shaken less if we were riding," Tonya says out of the side of her mouth.

"You and me both," Marni replies through a smile as the doors open.

The air leaves Connor and Hocks' lungs simultaneously. Everyone stands as the song changes and turns to watch as Marni Foster and Tonya Curston take their first step down the white fabric aisle.

It feels like an eternity before they make it to the end. Marni hands her bouquet off to Tonya and takes her place in front of Connor. Tonya, acting as her maid of honor, and Hocks, acting as Connor's best man, stands at opposite sides of the arch.

Connor holds his hands out and Marni places hers in his. His black cowboy hat shields his blue eyes until he swallows the lump in his throat and looks up.

"You look beautiful," he whispers, and a blush creeps across Marni's cheeks. A hush falls over the ceremony as Connor repeats his vows, followed by Marni. When they ask for the rings, Hocks pulls a ring box from his pocket.

Marni's fingers shake slightly as Connor slides her ring into place and brings her hand to his lips. Her stomach flips, and he lowers her hands.

"Do you Marni Foster take this man to be your lawfully wedded husband?"

"I do," she says, not an ounce of doubt in her body.

The judge nods. "And do you, Connor Curston, take this woman to be your lawfully wedded wife?"

"I absolutely do."

"I now pronounce you husband and wife. You may kiss your bride," the judge announces, and Connor pulls her into him. He tips her head back and wraps an arm around her waist. The crowd cheers as he presses his lips to hers, solidifying their promise to love each other and prove it every day.

"Now," the judge says with a slight chuckle. "I've never done this before, but you folks are getting a two for one deal. Tonya, Hocks," he says, gesturing to the next couple. Marni takes the wedding bouquets while the grooms switch places.

Tonya shimmies in her dress as she takes Hocks' shaky hands. "Loosen up, Stud. You look like you might crack," she murmurs, and those attendees closest to the front chuckle.

"All you have to do is repeat after me, son," the judge jokes.

"Actually, I have something I want to say," Hocks says and Tonya tilts her head, confused.

"What are you doing?" she whispers and he winks.

"Darlin', I didn't know what my future held most of my life, living day by day just trying to survive. Then I started working on your family's ranch and found a routine that I grew to love. Now I get to plant roots and grow old with you on that piece of heaven. I wake up looking forward to the day instead of dreading it, and I owe all that to you. You're my world, Tonya Curston, and I'll prove myself to you every minute of every day and I'll never stop loving you."

A collective awh sounds throughout the barn and Tonya leans in, pressing her lips to his.

"Show off," Connor jokes and Marni giggles.

"Hold on now, we're getting ahead of ourselves," the judge teases and Tonya pulls back. "Do you, Hocks--"

"Hell yeah, I do," Hocks interrupts and Tonya laughs, squeezing his hand with aching cheeks.

The judge raises his brows and turns to Tonya. "Do you Tonya--"

"Abso-fucking-lutely," she squeals, cutting him off.

"Tonya," Stacy hisses, and the crowd cackles.

"Well, you heard them folks. For the first time, I am proud to introduce Mr. and Mrs. Connor Curston and Mr. and Mrs. Hocks Curston!"

Tonya cheers, raising her and Hocks' intertwined fingers and everyone erupts to their feet.

Connor sweeps Marni up into his arms as they walk down the aisle following Tonya and Hocks, who practically run to the end.

"We did it!" Tonya squeals when they're the only ones inside the small room while everyone else sets up the reception area. She jumps into Hocks' arms and kisses him, not caring about her makeup at all.

"We sure did, darlin' and now you're stuck with me forever," Hocks responds, spinning his wife around in a small circle.

"We did it," Marni parrots, softer and gazes up at Connor, who places a hand on her stomach.

"And this next part of our lives will be the best yet," he says.

Four people whose lives looked so bleak and hopeless at times found their happily ever afters. Each has faced some of the darkest times of their lives and came out stronger for it. In each other, they found something they didn't know existed, someone who accepts them and their haunted memories.

And they're on to their next chapter in life.

Afterword

If somehow you read this and got to the end and thought 'who are these people so I can read more', welcome to the Chantellverse.

Welcome to a wild ride of spicy cowboy romance books where I put my characters through hell to get their happy endings.

About the author

Lacy Chantell resides in Kentucky and owns a small business. She is a mom of two toddlers and lives on the family farm with her husband. She loves to read all genres, ride her horses, hiking, pretty much anything outdoors. Inspiration hits her everywhere she goes for new book ideas, and she is excited to keep telling stories for others to enjoy. Romance and Fantasy are her favorite genres to write, and she loves to put her characters through hell for them to get their happy ending in the end.

Follow her on her social media accounts or join her newsletter to keep up with releases and her future works.

Also by

Lacy Chantell – Cowboy Romance

Curston Ranch Series

Wild Heart–Book One

Tattered Heartstrings–Book Two

Wildflowers and Wild Horses–Book Three

A Curston Ranch Christmas – A Christmas Novella

Langley Ranch Series

The Reason Why - Book One

Dreaming of Dahlias – Cowboy Romance Standalone

Lacie Chanel – Dark and Taboo Romance

Seeing Double – Why Choose Romance

The Games We Play – Stalker Dark Romance

Intracoastal Waters – A Dark Billionaire Romance releases Feb 8th

www.ingramcontent.com/pod-product-compliance
Ingram Content Group UK Ltd.
Pitfield, Milton Keynes, MK11 3LW, UK
UKHW041851190726
13854UKWH00002B/838